The Secret of The Gypsy Queen

Written By
Brian Dunning

Illustrated by
Jesse Horn

FOR JESSE

Enjoy this tale with the accompanying
Music and Narration

http://skeptoid.com/audio/skeptoid-4300.mp3

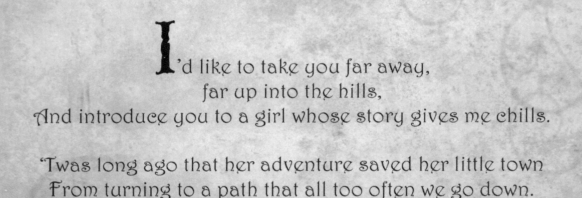

I'd like to take you far away,
far up into the hills,
And introduce you to a girl whose story gives me chills.

'Twas long ago that her adventure saved her little town
From turning to a path that all too often we go down.

The little town was prosperous,
and all its people happy.
The scissormaker's name was Opa
(German for Grandpappy).

His little Ilse loved him so.
She ran his grinding mill.
One day she came into the shop,
and found him standing still.

"Opa, You've got a scarf tied o'er your eyes
Opa, You cannot see, you realize?
Dear Opa, what's the point of that?
You cannot see a thing
You've done no work,
you also look just like a ding-a-ling.
I'd say the shop's a mess if I were one to moralize.
Please Opa, won't you tell me why that scarf's
tied o'er your eyes?"

"It's called an Überscarf, it is; a wondrous new invention.
It makes things go away,
the things that cause me hypertension.
If stocks are low,
the Überscarf will hide that from my sight.
If I can't see a problem, well then, everything's all right.
When the shop's untidy, or the pantry shelves are bare,
My splendid Überscarf will keep me blissf'lly unaware."

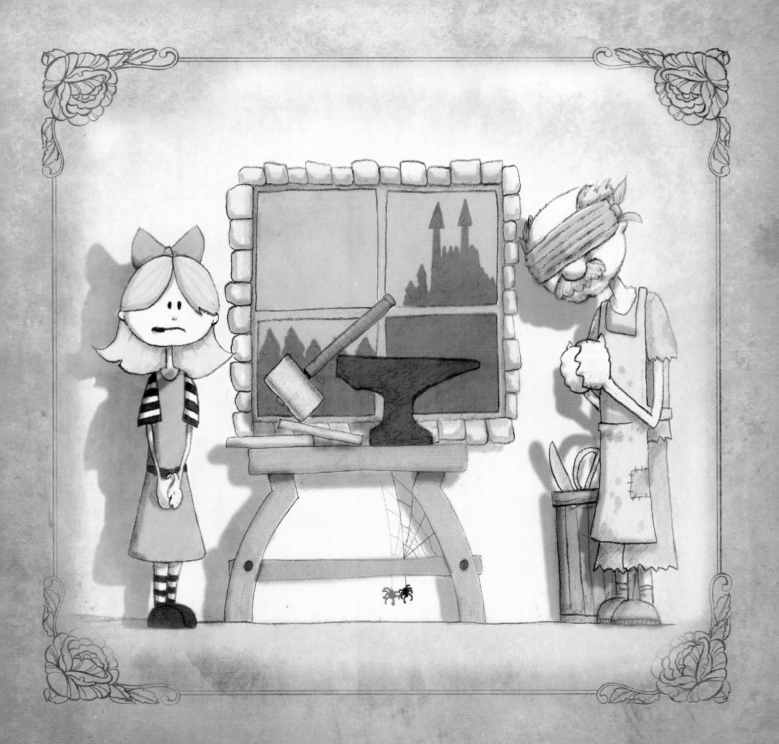

"Of all I've heard, that is the most ridiculous today.
Who told you covering your eyes makes troubles go away?"

"Why Ilse dear I'll tell you, just a moment to recount it,
A friendly rat was selling them at market, all discounted.
He told me how it works, he said my troubles would be banished;
And once he tied it round my head, well sure enough, they vanished!
But one thing more convinced me of the Überscarf's cachet:
It's not made here, exotic scarves are crafted far away.
The Gypsy Queen of Großerkopf creates them in her castle,
Her servant rats distribute them to spare the buyer hassle."

"The Gypsy Queen, I've heard of her
So she's behind this mess.
The Gypsy Queen, that swindler
I'll find her nonetheless.
I'll ask her what these Überscarves are really all about,
She sold my Opa rubbish, she and I will have it out.
The Großerkopf is far away, but in my line of sight;
The journey's long, but off I go. I'll try to make things right."

So Ilse packed a satchel and she started on her way.
Though Opa told her not to, Ilse chose to disobey.

She hadn't gone a furlong when she came upon a gent
Whose hard-earned money also on an Überscarf was spent.
He couldn't see, and so he made his way along the road
By holding to a fence, and step by step was how he strode.

"The Mayor has an Überscarf
Tied all around his head.
The Mayor has an Überscarf
How far has this thing spread?

Oh Mayor, please be careful for you cannot see the lane:
We cannot have you falling down and ending up in pain.
Please sir, may I ask you why you're covering your eyes?
Are you sure it helps you govern? Are you sure it's very wise?"

"It's the greatest thing," the mayor said, and groped to find the rails,
"I see no beggars wanting food, no outlaws in our jails.
I see no trash or disarray. My vision's been unleashed;
This Überscarf has opened up my eyes and shown me nicht!
I'm going now to make a brand new city proclamation:
An Überscarf for every single person in the nation!"

"This problem's spreading far and wide
Much farther than I knew
The mayor has a level head
But he has bought one too.
It seems that everyone in town has bought this silly hoax!
Hello, what's happ'ning at the home of these nice village folks?"

And there they were: A man and wife doing naught but standing there,
Wearing Überscarves and with their house in disrepair.
Their cottage doors were open and the upstairs windows too,
And into waiting wagons rats tossed bags of revenue.
They walked right past the family as they carried 'way their swag,
And tipped their hats and waved and simply told them "Guten tag."

"So that's the Gypsy Queen's design,
To make the folks content
Then send her rats to clean them out
Of house and home and rent!
Call the crier! Raise alarms from every house and tower,
It must be fast, it must be soon, for late now is the hour!
I'm headed now for Großerkopf to tell that Gypsy Queen
Exactly what I think of her and her disgusting scheme!"

She ran along the road until she reached the edge of town,
But then she struck a roadblock manned by soldiers from the Crown.
I'm sure you've guessed it:
Überscarves were what the soldiers wore.

One spoke: "You shall not pass this gate,"
but there was something more:

A group of rats came out and gathered round the little girl,
One well-dressed rat stepped up,
and did an Überscarf unfurl.

"My charming Ilse", said the rat,
"don't knock it 'til you've tried it.
I know you'll love your Überscarf.
Your worry is misguided."

"You keep your Überscarf, you rats.
I will not buy your scam;
I'll not add to your sales stats
For skeptical I am.
My business isn't here with you, so let me make this plain:
I'm headed for the Großerkopf; good day, Auf Wiedersehen!"

Ilse sprang away, the blinded soldiers bonked their heads.
Through the trees she ran and dashed through groves and riverbeds.
The soldiers tripped and stumbled and the rats all fell behind,
So Ilse got away, and then the Großerkopf she spied.

A grueling journey brought her to the mighty mountain's feet,
And up she climbed until she reached the Gypsy Queen's retreat.

Into the castle's dark she crept, and came upon a scene:
A great stone hall, all full of rats at work with sewing machines.
And then, as Ilse watched, a fearsome presence soon appeared:

The Gypsy Queen herself was there! But Ilse only sneered;
Then she leaped into the hall and vaulted 'cross a stone ravine,
She dodged some rats and ran right up to face the daunting Queen!

"So you are she
Quite a spree
Quite a sales jamboree
New meaning you have given "popularity"
You say it's great
Worth the wait
You say it sets the whole world straight
But all it really does is hide reality."

"Oh that's not all it does, my dear," so spake the Gypsy Queen,
"You've seen just the iceberg's tip of my corrupt machine!"

Then giant gates swung open and at least a hundred score
Of her illicit, dirty, thieving rats came marching through the door.
They pulled great wagons, piled high with booty, loot, and plunder
For all across the kingdom, every fortune lay asunder.

"It's a trick!
It's a trick!
Your whole plan was just a trick!
You gave them Überscarves so you could rob them blind.
You must stop!
You must stop!
I am going to make you stop.
I will stop you any way that I can find!"

"Oh I think not," the Queen remarked, and very wryly smiled
As half a dozen rats lunged out and grabbed the little child!

Ilse saw the world go dark as something masked her eyes.
Her Überscarf was fastened tight when someone yanked its ties.

"Take it off! Take it off! Do you hear me? Take it off!
Take it off and let me go, you've had your fun.
Let me go! Let me go! Are you going to let me go?
Let me go or you'll regret what you have done!"

"So tell me, little Ilse," asked the Queen, "what do you see?
You see no rats, you see no strife, you see no thievery.
Is not my Überscarf the finest thing you've ever worn?"

But Ilse wasn't buying it. No, Ilse wasn't torn.
She reached into her pocket with a hand that still was free.

"Tell me, Ilse," asked the Queen again, "what do you see?"

"I see all I can!"

Out came Opa's scissors! With a single snip it fell,
Her eyes flashed bright! The rats jumped back,
the Gypsy Queen as well.
She jumped to where some soldiers stood on guard across the way,
And with a flash of steel she cut their Überscarves away.

"I see all
Big and small
I see everything you do
And I'm going to make sure everyone sees too.
With this pair
of scissors fair
I'll make everyone aware
Gypsy Queen, your termination's overdue!"

The soldiers chased the rats, who scattered jumbled and afraid,
And every Überscarf that Ilse saw fell to her blade.
She found the road to town and took it, cutting left and right,
A hundred Überscarves were sliced, a hundred saw the light.
"Throw your Überscarves away
See what they have done
Witness now this exposé
See the smoking gun
Your pantries all are empty and your valuables are gone
Drive these rats away, because the Überscarf's a con!"

And every person rubbed his eyes, and saw the horrid rats.
They chased the rats away from town with sticks and brooms and bats.
They saw their empty cupboards and their tempers were unbound.
They followed Ilse, shredding every Überscarf around.
Ilse made it home and found her Opa under weather.

"Oh Ilse, I'm so frozen, for I cannot find my sweater.
I'm nearly starved as well because I couldn't find the bacon;
My Überscarf is all I have that hasn't me forsaken."

Ilse gently raised her scissors, snipped that scarf away.
Opa blinked and looked around, and all was A-OK.

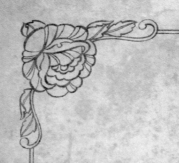

"Opa
You had a scarf tied o'er your eyes

Opa
It never worked, you realize?

When someone promises you magic and they want your cash,
And all they give you is a trinket, it's just balderdash.
Whether junk or juice or jewelry or a hologram,
There's always someone selling something that is just a sham.

Opa
You only lost a little bit, but

Opa
You never will lose me."

Now once again, the village scissormaker works his craft,
His diligent assistant grinds a blade on every shaft.
But Ilse and her Opa make up quite the crafty pair:
Just try to rip them off. Come on, try it. I dare.

The End

Brian Dunning is a writer and producer who specialises in the debunking of pseudoscience. He has hosted a weekly podcast, Skeptoid, since 2006 and has also written articles and books, and produced a TV series on the subject.
skeptoid.com

Jesse Horn is a children's writer and illustrator. When he is not attempting to hide the skeletons kept in his closet, he is busy running from them.
awickedworld.com

98646938R00020

Made in the USA
Columbia, SC
04 July 2018